Little Pussycat

By Margaret Wise Brown
Pictures by Leonard Weisgard

Originally published under the title PUSSY WILLOW

A GOLDEN BOOK • NEW YORK

Western Publishing Company, Inc., Racine, Wisconsin 53404

W9-CBC-845

Copyright © 1951 by Western Publishing Company, Inc. Copyright renewed 1979. All rights reserved. Printed in the U.S.A. No part of this book may be reproduced or copied in any form without written permission from the publisher. GOLDEN®, GOLDEN & DESIGN®, A LITTLE GOLDEN BOOK®, and A GOLDEN BOOK® are trademarks of Western Publishing Company, Inc. ISBN 0-307-02062-2   R S T

ONCE there was a little pussycat not much bigger than a pussywillow. He was just as soft and gray and furry as those little flowers clinging to the branches all about him in the early Spring. So he named himself Pussy Willow.

It was a wild green world that he was born into. A forest of wild flowers grew above him. Some things were bigger than he was. And some things were smaller than he was. And he wondered at such little things.

Suddenly a bug jumped out of that wild green world and up to him.

"Where are you good to bite?" asked the bug.

"Nowhere and not at all," said Pussy Willow, and he rolled the bug back in the grass with his soft fur foot.

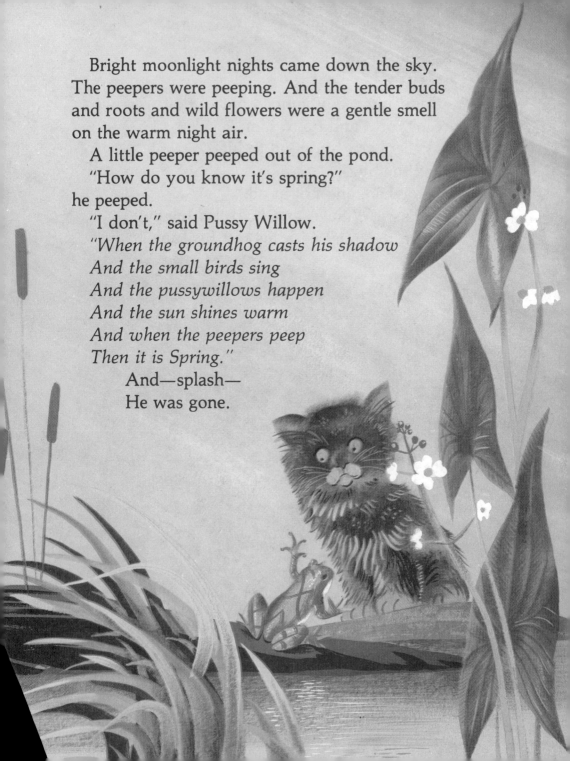

Bright moonlight nights came down the sky.
The peepers were peeping. And the tender buds
and roots and wild flowers were a gentle smell
on the warm night air.

A little peeper peeped out of the pond.

"How do you know it's spring?"
he peeped.

"I don't," said Pussy Willow.
"When the groundhog casts his shadow
And the small birds sing
And the pussywillows happen
And the sun shines warm
And when the peepers peep
Then it is Spring."
And—splash—
He was gone.

A deer mouse came softly out of the forest
and tickled Pussy Willow on the nose.

"How odd," she said. "A cat not much
bigger than a mouse.

"Little fat shadow," said the mouse, "come
home with me and live in my house."

"*Kerchew!* I am not a shadow. Shadows
don't sneeze—*Kerchew!*"

Pussy Willow gave such a big sneeze that it
blew the mouse over.

Time passed: hours and minutes and nig
and days. And Pussy Willow grew more fur
   Wild strawberries bloomed about him.
   Green grasshoppers hopped over him.
   Suddenly Pussy Willow looked up.
   His pussywillows were gone. Gone.
   Long yellow things and little green leaves
hung from the branches where his pussywillows
had been.
   Where had they gone?
   He would go and find them.
       And he would look until he found them again.

So off he went—

through moonlight
and
starlight

and thunder
and lightning

looking for his pussywillows.

He searched

through the day
and the night

and the wind
and the rain.

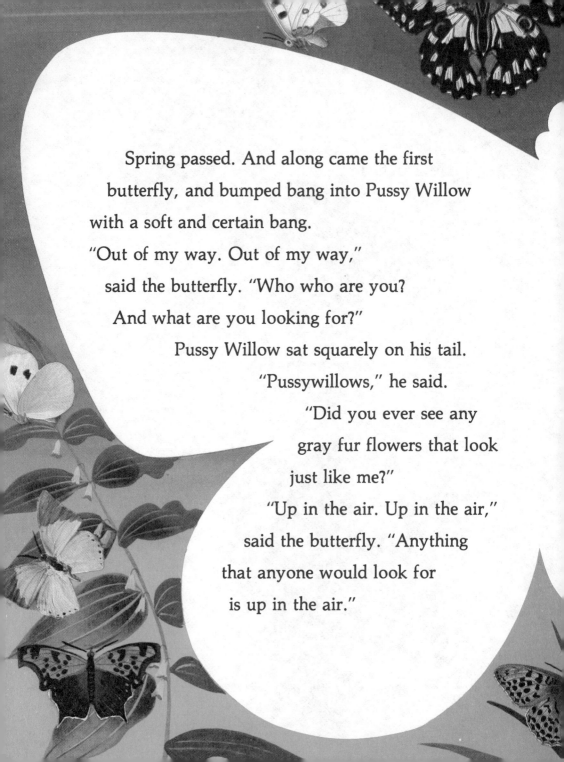

Spring passed. And along came the first
butterfly, and bumped bang into Pussy Willow
with a soft and certain bang.
"Out of my way. Out of my way,"
    said the butterfly. "Who who are you?
    And what are you looking for?"
        Pussy Willow sat squarely on his tail.
            "Pussywillows," he said.
                "Did you ever see any
                gray fur flowers that look
                just like me?"
                "Up in the air. Up in the air,"
            said the butterfly. "Anything
        that anyone would look for
        is up in the air."

So Pussy Willow climbed a tree and fell asleep
in a bird's nest. The birds came home and
found him warm and purring next to their eggs.
So they sat on him, too, and kept him warm.

Little friendly birds came out of the eggs and
grew up and learned to fly.

"Everything that anyone would ever look for
is up in the sky," they sang, and flew up.

Pussy Willow climbed all around the treetops, but he never learned to fly.

One day a bee flew by. "Who are you, and where shall I sting you?"

"Don't," said Pussy Willow. "But tell me, did you ever see any gray fur flowers that look just like me?"

"Sassafras," buzzed the bee. "Look in the garden."

So Pussy Willow climbed down into
a garden. And there he found cabbages
and roses, scarecrows, poppies, and
pink tiger lilies.

But no pussywillows.

He went up to a big fat cabbage.

"Did you ever see any little gray
fur flowers that look just like me?"

But the cabbage sat there in its great
green silence and never said a word.

Up popped a mole. "Anything that anyone would look for is always in a hole."

"In a carrot," said the rabbit.

"In a garden," buzzed the bee.

"In a smell," sniffed the skunk.

And the woodpecker pecked at a tree.

Pussy Willow hunted through moonlight
and sunlight and down by the sea. There he met
an old hermit crab. The hermit crab came
snapping out of his shell, waving all his claws.

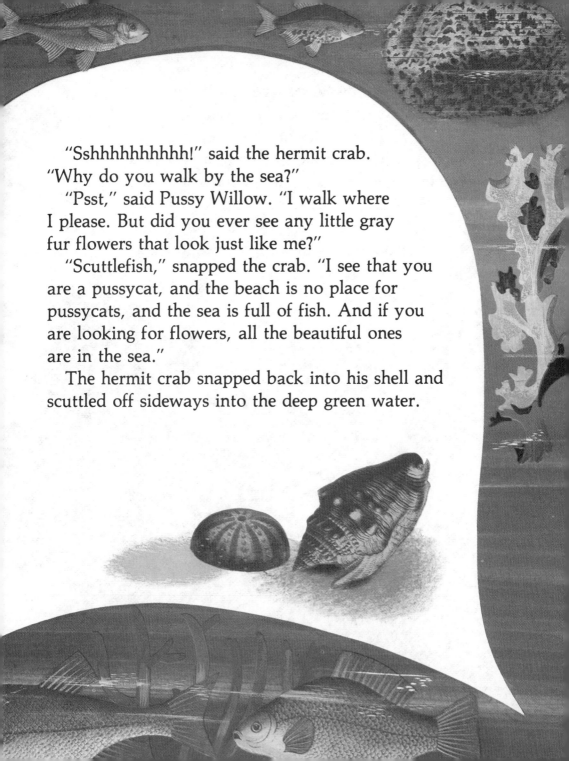

"Sshhhhhhhhh!" said the hermit crab. "Why do you walk by the sea?"

"Psst," said Pussy Willow. "I walk where I please. But did you ever see any little gray fur flowers that look just like me?"

"Scuttlefish," snapped the crab. "I see that you are a pussycat, and the beach is no place for pussycats, and the sea is full of fish. And if you are looking for flowers, all the beautiful ones are in the sea."

The hermit crab snapped back into his shell and scuttled off sideways into the deep green water.

So Pussy Willow wandered through purple asters
and goldenrod and pearly everlasting,
through blueberries and blackberries and
raspberries. But still he couldn't find his
lost pussywillows. The wind began to blow.
The leaves turned red and fell from the trees.
Nuts fell on Pussy Willow's head, and apples
dropped about him, with a loud
and sudden
pop.

Pussy Willow met
a red squirrel hiding acorns.

"Are you a nut?" asked the red squirrel.

"What do you think?" said Pussy Willow.
"Did you ever see a nut with whiskers and
pointed ears and a switching tail?

"I am a cat looking for pussywillows. Did you
ever see any little soft gray fur flowers that look
just like me?"

"Look under the leaves," said the red squirrel.
"Everything that anyone would look for is always
under the leaves."

The air grew colder. Snow fell. Pussy Willow
hunted through snowstorms and black branches
and across the shining ice. Until at last
he fell asleep, a very tired pussycat under
a thin-branched bush.

Pussy Willow took a little catnap. And
while he was asleep, something began
to happen on the branches high above him.

The sun shone warm, and he dreamed that
there was a soft purring in the air around him.
The groundhog came out of the ground.

And when he saw a little
cat in his shadow—*Thump!*
"Get out of my shadow,"
he said and
woke him up.

Then all the birds began to sing.
The redwing blackbird, the meadowlark,
and the bobolink whistled in the air.
The peepers in the pond began to peep.
It was Spring.
And when Pussy Willow uncurled
himself, there were his pussywillows.
For he had fallen asleep under a
pussywillow bush, and it had burst
into bloom above him.

"Everything that anyone would ever look for
is usually where they left it," hooted the owl.
"On a bush," sang the robin.
"In the sky," sang the lark.
"In a song
In the Spring
In the dark."
Then up popped Pussy Willow.
"Everything that anyone would ever look for
is usually where they find it,"
purred Pussy Willow.